Stella's Secret

Stella's Secret is dedicated to my family,
the whole beautiful lot. I am eternally grateful for your love and friendship.
I also dedicate this to little Finlay Blake and Sage Miles,
who left us all too soon, but who now embrace Stella's story fully with joy!

Lydia du Toit

Lydia and Francois du Toit live in South Africa.

I think my imagination for story telling started in my early childhood. We lived like gypsies in a caravan and travelled criss cross our beautiful country wherever my Pappa's work would take him. Long before any TV or even access to radio we invented stories and created places yet to be discovered at night around the campfires or in bed with Mamma's stories, taking us with her to Neverland. CS Lewis, and his Narnia stories as well as works of Elizabeth Goudge were some of my favorite bedside reading material. There is a world lying waiting in the child's mind and I hope that Stella's Secret will unlock a beautiful safe place for all who read and hear her.
www.mirrorword.net

Wendy Francisco

Wendy resides with her husband, singer/songwriter Don Francisco, in the mountains of Colorado where she has many animals, and continues to produce art, writings and music.
www.WendyFrancisco.com

My deepest thanks to the team that made this delightful read possible. Wendy Francisco, thank you for the months of labor and love to create these masterpieces of art. Jacqueline du Toit, all your hours to do the layout of Stella's Secret, thank you. Sean Osmond, helping us with final preparations for print and Kindle. Bess Rhoades for your encouragement and help with the editing. Thank you my darling husband and friend for more than 40 years, I see you on every page!

I am so grateful for the Mirror Message it has brought God into full view again, in you!

Thank you to all my translators:
Into Xhosa — Mongo Mbubulelo; Shona — Shelton Muduyaro; Afrikaans — Catrina Wessels; German — Monica Zurbruegg; Spanish — Carlos Solomon

El Secreto de Estela

Lydia du Toit - *Author*
Wendy Francisco - *Illustrator*

Published by Mirror Word Publishing

We have this treasure
where it was hidden all along,
in these frail skinsuits made of clay.
2 Corinthians 4:7 Mirror Bible

www.mirrorword.net

Stella's Secret

It was a beautiful spring day; the sun was shining like a big orange in the sky, and the wind was blowing music through the trees. (Can you hear it, too?)

"Caw, caw," cried a black crow from the branches. Stella looked up from her picnic blanket where she and Matilda were sitting in the shade of the oak tree.

"We'd better pack up now," said Stella to Matilda as she started folding up the picnic blanket and putting her juice bottle back into the basket. "I know it's a weekend, but today is a working day for me, and I have oh, so much to do..." she whispered as she picked up her rag doll, Matilda, and clasped her under her arm.

"Today I have to find God and I don't know who will help me look for Him.... Oh, Mr. Crow!" she called up into the tree, "Do you know where I can find God?"

Cedric the crow jumped to a branch just above her head. "Hello, Stella," he croaked. "I can fly quite high, Stella, over the trees and the mountaintops. I see lots of God every time but I have not found all of Him there."

Stella looked disappointed, but just before she could walk off, Mr. Crow continued: "Why don't we ask Farrell, the black eagle— he can fly much higher than I can. I know where he lives— up against that rock face," he said and pointed with his wings to the majestic Makulu Mountains in front of them.

"You wait here for me, Stella; I'll find him for you."

"Oh, thank you, Mr. Crow!"

Stella's Secret

Stella watched as her feathered friend disappeared into the sky and decided that maybe she should finish her sandwich and have her apple that Mommy had packed in her picnic. It was a beautiful day and Stella was doing what she loved the most, so she started singing her picnic song:

I love picnics out in the open
Having my sandwiches is so much fun
Sitting on the blanket in the shade of the oak trees
Can you hear the birds' song
Having a picnic in the sun

Suddenly a big black bird blocked the sun and landed in the tree in front of her.

Piercing eyes looked down at Stella over a gleaming yellow beak. His long legs were covered in pitch-black feathers that were shining in the sun and made his bright yellow claws look even bigger.

Stella shrieked with a mixture of fear and delight.

"Hello, Stella! I am sorry to have given you such a fright. I came right away after Cedric the Crow told me you needed my assistance for a rather important matter."

"Yes, yes," stuttered Stella. "I did send Cedric to find you, Mr. Farrell. I need to know from you..."

"Pardon me for interrupting you, dear lady— my name is not Farrell but Fastest Fearless Farrell, the Mighty Black Eagle!"

Stella's Secret

"Oh, I do apologize, Fastest Fearless Farrell," said Stella. "Please tell me, did you perhaps find God in your journeys?"

"Dear Stella," started Farrell, "may I call you just Stella?"

"Yes, please— do just call me Stella. Mommy calls me Stella Bella, and Daddy does, too, but I like just Stella."

"Well, Stella, I flew as high as my wings would take me— up, up and beyond. I saw streams and mighty rivers; hills and winding mountain ranges that look like a dragon's back from up high. I've seen snow peaked mountains and towns and cities and clouds floating underneath my talons. The views were magnificent. Hmmm....," he interrupted himself, "Have I shown you my talons, Stella?

Just have a look at them."

Stella looked in wonder at his claws that clasped the branch; one could see his bright yellow feet and long nails. She looked up at his head; the wind was blowing the feathers around his face like a crown. "A delightful and royal bird indeed," she thought.

"Oh, I saw rain clouds and snow clouds," he continued, "and clouds carrying lightning like a jewel-box glimmering in the sun; I saw so much, Stella Bella... oops... I saw so much of God, dear Stella, but I did not find all of Him— not even hiding somewhere in the great blue, blue sky."

Her face fell, and she sat down thoughtfully on the blanket. She looked up at Fastest Fearless Farrell.

"Thank you for all your trouble, Mr. Eagle. But don't worry— I know I will find Him somewhere."

As he took off in flight the branches and leaves made a rushing sound; she watched him disappear into the sky and heard him call back at her: "I know you'll find Him, Stella!"

Stella's Secret

The footpath in front of Stella was taking her through the tall poplar trees with their yellow autumn leaves rustling in the wind. Stella was so excited that she started running, Matilda clasped under her arm, the doll's head bouncing up and down with every step she took.

"Can you hear the waves too, Matilda?" she asked. The familiar little path soon had Stella on the soft white sand. With her shoes off and Matilda clasped tightly under her arm, Stella found her favorite rock pool and immediately put her feet in the cool water. The seagulls were flying overhead, squawking loudly; they too were enjoying the moment with Stella.

A big brown and orange speckled crab crawled from underneath a rock in front of her, apparently trying to sneak away. Stella was amazed that he could clamber sideways over the sand and rocks so smoothly.

"Why are you staring at me?" he asked her.

"Oh! I am so glad you're a talking crab!" said Stella. "I was just admiring your skill, climbing so fast over the rocks— and under water, too! I am looking to find all of God, Mr. Crab. Is He hiding in the ocean somewhere? Have you seen Him?" Stella asked.

"Oh, my goodness!" exclaimed the crab. "You are a very brave girl— aren't you scared to find God?"

''Oh no, Mr. Crab.''

"You can call me Caleb," he interrupted.

"Caleb, I'm not scared at all. He is powerful and wise and wonderful but I've never been afraid of him."

"But what if you had done something that you shouldn't have? Surely then you would be scared of Him, wouldn't you....?"

Stella's Secret

Stella stooped down with her head close to the rock on which Caleb had made himself comfortable.

"I am never scared of Him," she insisted.

"Did you notice that I have eyes that pop out on the sides of my head and that I can look in front of me as well as behind me at the same time?" he asked. He moved closer to her so she could see.

"Brave Stella, I would have seen all of God if He was hiding anywhere in the wide ocean. Unfortunately, that means, my dear," he continued, "that you will have to look for Him somewhere else— and I hope He is as good as you think He is!"

A big beautiful seagull landed on the rock next to Stella, making Caleb scurry for shelter under the water in a wink. But this seagull was not interested in Caleb for her next meal: She was on a mission, sent by Cedric the Crow.

"Cedric has sent me, dear Stella. He is quite concerned and wanted to know if you have found all of God yet?"

"Oh, thank you! How kind of him. Do tell Cedric that I will most certainly let him know once I have found God's favorite place to stay," Stella told her beautiful white-feathered friend.

Sally the seagull looked intently at Stella, whose feet were dangling in the rock pool, her hat pulled so tightly over her mop of dark curls that one could hardly see her face- just her soft red cheeks.

"Maybe He is not as far off as you think, Stella," she said, and with her strong, neatly feathered wings lifted herself effortlessly into the blue sky, dancing a delightful wing-dance with the other gulls.

"I had better be going home now," Stella whispered to Caleb, who was still hiding under a rock in the water, but could be seen peeping at her.

Stella brushed Matilda's wet hair out of her face so she could see her bright blue button eyes and red button nose and mouth shining in the sun. "Oh, Matilda— I'll have to wash your hair when we get home," she sighed.

Stella's Secret

After school on Wednesday, Mommy picked Stella up at the school gate but instead of going home they went to town. Mommy wanted to see if they could find Stella a new pair of shoes since Wednesday was market day. Stella loved the market. She loved to walk through the tables with lovely fresh fruit and homemade bread and jam and all kinds of homemade delights. Her favorite stall was Mollie's Flower Table. It was covered with bunches of mixed heath and iris and gladioli and soft pink and bright red roses, all neatly stacked in buckets of water. Mollie was busy helping a customer with some flowers, and Stella's heart jumped with joy when she saw who it was.

"Father Jacob!" she called.

"Oh, Stella Bella!" he called back. "It's wonderful to see you. Come and help me pick some flowers for Aunt Mary; it will be her birthday on Friday and I know that she will love them even more if you help me pick them."

Soon the two were lost in a world of flowers. Stella's arms were so full of bright blue and red and green and yellow flowers that one could hardly see her face.

"Father Jacob," she said, "I am extra happy to see you because I think you will know the answer to my secret quest."

Stella's Secret

Father Jacob took an empty flower bucket, turned it over, and sat down on it low so he could look Stella in the eyes.

"Where will I find all of God?" she began. "I have been looking and asking around because I really need to know this secret." She proceeded to tell him of Mr. Crow and Farrell and Caleb and Sally. "Could He possibly be hiding in the parish somewhere— or maybe in that very tall steeple on the church?"

"Oh, no, Stella," said Father Jacob with a sigh. "I don't know where He is hiding, but I do know that it's not anywhere in the church building. I am there on Sundays, Mondays, Tuesdays— oh, almost every day of the week, day and night, and He is not hiding there.

I have felt His presence there... but then I have also felt His closeness in my car and in the grocer's shop, too. But, Stella, you mustn't stop looking! I know you will find Him."

Father Jacob got up slowly from his seat on the bucket and walked to Mollie to pay her for the flowers. She, in turn, came to Stella with a lovely little posy of bright red and yellow flowers.

"This is for you, dear Stella," she grinned. Stella took the posy from Mollie and tugged on Mollie's skirt so she could kneel down for a hug. Mollie looked down and cupped her face in her hands— "My, oh my," 'she laughed, "you look just like your beautiful mommy, Stella. You have that same mop of hair and dimples and that twinkle in your eyes!"

Stella's Secret

Stella found Mommy still busy at the food stalls and decided to wait for her on the soft green grass, in the shade of an old oak tree covered with soft green leaves. It was so beautiful and cool that Stella lay down on her back. Suddenly there was a movement under the grass next to her. Stella sat up, surprised to find a mole that had just popped out from underneath the ground with some sand still stuck on his whiskers.

"Hello, Stella," said Sherlock the Mole.

"You gave me a little fright, Mr. Mole," said Stella.

"Oh, I didn't mean to do that, Stella. I just wanted to pop up from my underground world to feel some lovely sunshine for a change," he chuckled.

"Mr. Mole, you are really amazing. Digging deep into the earth and creating furrows and tunnels for miles and miles on end!"

"That's me!" called Sherlock. There is nothing that can hide from me underneath the ground. If it's there, I'll find it!"

"Oh Mr. Mole, this is wonderful news! Tell me, did you perhaps find God hiding somewhere in the dark underground?"

"Why, my goodness, dear Stella, off course He is here.... and He is also in the blue sky and greenest trees and biggest rivers and deepest ocean: but I don't think those are His favorite hiding place.

Now, don't you think for a minute, dear Stella," he continued bravely, "that because I am blind I cannot see. I see with the whiskers on my nose and my nostrils, and my toes and my ears. I see with all of me, Stella! Humans are weird creatures to think that they can only see with their eyes. Silly thoughts!" he said as he disappeared right into the hole where he came from, leaving Stella staring at the grass...

See with more than our eyes? she pondered curiously.

Stella's Secret

It was Stella's turn to clear the table after dinner and fetch the old leather Bible from the mantelpiece. Grandpa read them the story of Jesus and His disciples, where Jesus was telling them that He was going to leave them. Stella also felt the disciples' concern. Why couldn't he just stay? she wondered.

Grandpa's gruff voice could also be amazingly soft and kind. "You will not see Me with your eyes but I will always be with you, closer than your breath," he continued to read.

Jesus and Sherlock both talked about seeing with other eyes, Stella thought to herself.

School got out early on Friday, and Stella and Matilda went to the sea; she walked on the soft white sand. Stella looked for Caleb in the rock pool where they last met, but he wasn't there.

His long-legged octopus friend told Stella that Caleb was busy preparing a home for his new wife and needed all his time to make the seaweed carpets and coral windows. Stella stayed around a bit, looking for sea anemones; she counted eight in the pond: soft blue and yellow and pink ones dancing with their fingers in the water.

Stella's Secret

The path home was a happy one for Stella, through the oak forest and past Aunty Jamie's wooden cabin. There's smoke rising from the chimney, so she must be home, thought Stella excitedly. She turned from the footpath and ran to the door.

"Aunty Jamie, Aunty Jamie, are you home?" Stella called. She remembered that Jamie was a little hard of hearing and called again, then stuck her head through the kitchen window. There she saw her, sitting at the table by the fireplace, reading. Stella imagined that what Aunty Jamie was reading must have been very beautiful because her face was shining and big tears were running down her wrinkled cheeks.

"Aunty Jamie, may I come in?" Stella called. "I am so happy to see you and you have such a lovely fire going and I have to tell you something!" The words spilled out of Stella's mouth excitedly.

"Hello Stella, dear child! So much excitement, I see— come and tell me all!"

Stella pulled out a chair that was under the old oak table and sat right next to Aunty Jamie.

Looking at her eyes, Stella thought that they were bluer than the ocean she had just seen.

Pools of turquoise love looked back at Stella.

"I have just baked some bread— shall we have a slice with jam and tea while you tell me your exciting stories, dear Stella?"

"I would love that, but before you get up, please tell me what you were reading that made your face shine like the sun?"

Aunty Jamie was moved by Stella's observation.

"Stella, it's the biggest secret I've ever discovered, and I just found it today! The secret was hiding on these pages that I have read so often, but today the words jumped out of the pages and fell like magic into my heart. Did you know words could do that, Stella? Words are stronger than cannons.

Words are like seeds lying under the soil, and when the rain comes, they burst out of the ground and grow into beautiful plants."

Stella's Secret

$\mathcal{S}$he continued, while cutting the steaming hot bread on the board and adding her homemade jelly.

"I'm reading God's story about you and me in the Bible. It reminded me of a couple of other stories.

Do you remember the lovely story of the ugly duckling that looked in the pool of water and saw a beautiful swan looking back at him?

"Oh, yes, I love that story," Stella replied.

"Remember how he discovered that he was actually the beautiful swan and not the ugly duckling?

There's a similar story where the baby lion gazed at his reflection in a pool of water and saw his daddy looking back at him," Jamie continued.

"I love that story, too!" Stella blurted out.

"Well, that is very much like what I read today." Jamie leaned forward and looked intently at Stella. "When we look deep inside our hearts, guess what we see? We see God Himself looking right back at us! He made us to look just like Him!

"Is that possible, Aunty Jamie?" stammered Stella. "Is it really possible that God's inside of me?"

"Yes Stella, He has always been there— and He loves being God in you, Stella. In fact, it's His very favorite place to live!

"You know what else this means, Stella?"

Stella could hardly contain herself. Her eyes were as wide as saucers, and her feet were arched half way to tiptoe.

"This means that you are the beautiful swan. You are the strong lion. You are God's image!

How wonderful is that?" she said boldly. "You can see God in you every time you look in the mirror!

With that, Aunty Jamie broke out into such joyous laughter that Stella jumped to her feet and laughed, too.

Stella's Secret

"Oh, my goodness, Aunty Jamie! I've been looking for God everywhere....in the ocean, under theground, in the sky, in a church building. But I never thought to look inside!" Stella made a little danceof joy and sat down on the kitchen floor, flinging her arms in the air with a shriek of delight.

Running home, Stella noticed that the poppies had opened and their bright red faces were waving in the wind.

Aunty Jamie's words were ringing in her head like the peal of church bells on a crisp Sundaymorning:

God lives in me!
 I look just like Him!
  I see Him when I look in the mirror!
   I'm His favorite place to be!
    "I think you know it, too!" she shouted at the flowers as she ran by.

✎ the end ✎

CPSIA information can be obtained
at www.ICGtesting.com
Printed in the USA
BVHW010947110723
667065BV00002B/35